ROSCO THE RASCAL
EASTER ADVENTURE

Rosco the Rascal #7

By Shana Gorian

Illustrations by Deidre Gorian
Cover Art by Josh Addessi

CONTENTS

CHAPTER 1
SPRING CHICKENS

Six fluffy, yellow chicks strutted about the new pen in the McKendrick's backyard as Rosco, the family's German shepherd, looked on. *They're adorable!* thought Rosco. *I want to play with them!*

Ten-year-old James and his sister, seven-year-old Mandy, had built a chicken coop last week with their father. Today, Dad had brought home the baby chicks that would make it their home. It was a sunny day in April, and the peeps were just over two weeks old.

"They're so cute!" Mandy exclaimed for the third time in five minutes, scooping one up in her hands. "This is going to be the best

Easter ever!"

The little chick peeped, and Mandy smiled.

The holiday was only a week away, and so was the big Easter egg hunt. James and Mandy couldn't wait, but Mandy had been begging her father to get backyard chickens for months.

She studied the chicks' little, clawed feet. "Now all we need are some baby bunnies, and it'll feel like Easter all the time around here."

The McKendrick family didn't live on a farm. They lived in the suburbs, with sidewalks out front and a simple, grassy yard out back.

"Don't get any big ideas, Mandy. Six chickens, plus a dog—that's more than enough pets." Dad grinned. "Plus, baby chicks grow up. They don't stay this little and cute forever."

"Yes, but then the hens lay eggs," Mandy said, "and I'll collect them! It'll be like an Easter egg hunt everyday!"

James laughed. Rosco grinned.

"That's true," said Dad.

"So if these aren't feathers, what is this fluffy stuff called?" Mandy asked, stroking the back of the chick she held. "Is it yellow fur? It's so soft."

James carefully set one chick down and picked up another. "It's not fur. It's called *down*." The baby bird opened its tiny beak and let out another peeping sound. "Eventually, they'll lose the down when their feathers grow in."

"Oh." Mandy said, surprised. "How long does that take?"

"A few weeks." James stroked the chick's head.

"And *down* here is where the heat lamp will go," said Dad, grinning as he bent over and reached inside the coop to attach the lamp to a wired stand. Dad was setting up a heat lamp in the coop so the chicks would stay warm. They'd need it for a few weeks, before their feathers grew in.

Mandy had filled up their feeding tray and drinking water. James had covered the floor of the coop in a thick layer of straw.

Rosco paced around the coop, trying to get a better look at each of the tiny birds. Mandy was right—they were really cute. He stopped and stared at them, panting eagerly.

"Settle down, Rosco," said James. "You'll make them nervous."

"Oh, he's okay." Dad glanced at the dog. "He's just excited."

Mandy glanced at Rosco and set her chick in the pen with the others, where it immediately pecked at the grass. "Do chickens really eat bugs?"

"They sure do." Dad stood up and grabbed the sack of chicken food sitting on the ground. "Bugs are a great source of protein. But for now, they'll mostly just eat this. It's called mash." He poured some into the feeder.

Mandy laughed at the word. "Mash."

Dad picked up one of the chicks and

4

placed it inside the coop. "Yes, mash, and it will be your job to make sure they have enough food and water. James, it'll be your job to clean out the straw in the coop and refill it so it stays fresh."

James nodded. "Got it."

"Okay, kids, it's time to put the chicks inside the coop so they don't get cold."

"Okay," said Mandy. "There you go," she said to the chick, placing it inside the little red house. "Safe and warm."

"Dad, are you sure Rosco won't bother them?" Mandy asked.

Rosco's tongue hung out eagerly, and he licked his chops.

Dad glanced at Rosco. "I doubt it, but it's a good idea to keep an eye on him. You never know with dogs, even one as friendly as he is. Better to be safe than sorry."

James and Mandy gathered the rest of the chicks and put them back in the coop. Dad switched on the heat lamp.

Rosco finally stopped pacing and watched. He was excited to have more pets around, even if they'd be living outside. Dad didn't need to worry about him bothering these little critters, either. He'd make sure they were safe, even when the kids were off at school.

Dad closed the gate to the coop. "Okay, everyone, let's go finish that homework, and don't forget to wash your hands."

***

The next evening, after dinner, the kids were playing in their rooms while Rosco lounged on his doggie bed near the front door. The weather had been comfortable for springtime, and Mom hadn't yet closed the window in the kitchen.

Rosco's ears perked as something rustled outside in the bushes. He sat up quickly and heard it again. He rushed to a lower window where he could look into the backyard. What was out there? Something—that was for sure!

It was growing darker outside by the minute. Rosco strained his eyes and saw movement near the chicken coop. He saw a long tail and four legs. It was a coyote, sniffing around, wasn't it? He barked fiercely. "Ruff, ruff!"

He had to scare it away from the helpless, little chicks out there, even if they were safe, for now, inside the coop. Who knew if the clever coyote could find a way in? Rosco barked some more, and finally, the animal turned and gazed in Rosco's direction. Rosco growled.

"What is it, boy?" James called, hopping down the stairs.

In the next moment, Rosco watched the coyote dash around the side of the house, but would it leave for good? He'd better go and make sure.

Rosco ran to the front window and continued to bark, watching as the coyote trotted out of the front yard. *Don't come back, either!* Rosco thought. The curious creature would have to understand that the chicken coop was protected by a guard dog—a fierce one. The coyote had better stay away!

Mandy finally hurried down the staircase. She and James squeezed in next to Rosco at the window as he peered anxiously down the street, but the quiet coyote had already disappeared into the dusk.

"I don't see anything," she said. "What was he barking at?"

"I don't know. I didn't see anything,

either," said James.

Mandy turned to Rosco. "Silly, Rosco. There's nothing out there. You must be imagining things."

Rosco gazed back at her. They didn't understand. He sighed.

Oh, well. It didn't matter. The coyote was gone, and the chicks were safe—at least for now.

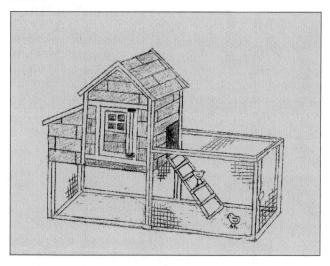

CHAPTER 2
GUARD DOG

The birds chirped and the bees buzzed, as James and Mandy played with the chicks a few days later. This time, Rosco circled the little fence around the coop with excitement. The chicks were so much fun to watch. He wished he could get in the pen and peck at the ground with them, but he was far too big. He might even step on one if he did.

Mandy eyed him nervously. "I know what Dad said, James, but do you think Rosco would ever hurt them?" She reached inside the coop for the water container. It was time to dump it out and refill it with fresh water. "Like—if we left him alone with them?"

James looked thoughtful. "Hmm. I don't

think so, but I guess it's possible." He glanced at Rosco, who stopped circling the fence long enough to sit down and pant. "He doesn't look like he'd hurt them, though."

Mandy nodded. "You're right."

Of course I won't hurt them, thought Rosco. How could he show the kids he could be trusted?

Maybe he could do his best to mind his manners? That should help.

Mandy took the feeding tray from the coop. "I'll be right back. I might as well fill up the mash when I fill up the water. Be a good boy, Rosco." She disappeared around the side of the house. The large sack of food was in the garage.

James opened the gate and took out one of the chicks. He held it and set it down in the grass. Two other chicks wandered out of the covered pen to join the first one. James watched them pecking at the grass, enjoying a little freedom outside the pen.

Mom called from the kitchen. "James,

can you come here for a moment, please? I need a little help with something."

"Coming, Mom!" he called. He scooped up the chicks, one by one, and placed them back inside the pen then pushed on the gate.

"James!" Mom called again.

"On my way, Mom!" He looked at Rosco. "Stay here, boy, and be good. I'll be right back." He hurried inside the house.

Rosco stayed, just as James had commanded, but James hadn't completely closed the gate. Soon, three of the little chicks had squeezed through the opening and wandered back out into the open. *Uh-oh.* Now what should he do?

For starters, he'd better keep them from getting away. He followed them as they circled around the outside of the coop.

Only a few moments later, Rosco noticed movement above. He looked up into the bright blue sky where a hawk circled overhead. *Oh no!* thought Rosco. *They're not safe from hawks out here!*

Hawks were known for stealing small animals, even fully-grown chickens, right off of the ground, in broad daylight. A baby chick would be far too easy to grab.

The chicks were completely unprotected. What should he do now? He had no time to guide them to the safety of the open gate or to convince them to go inside, if they'd even follow him.

"Ruff, ruff!" he barked. He glared up at the hawk. No hawk was going to steal even one of these chicks, if he had anything to say about it.

As Rosco barked and the hawk circled, the chicks ran to one wall of the pen and huddled together for comfort. He only hoped none of the other chicks would come out. They didn't even know what kind of danger they were facing out here.

Rosco continued to growl and bark at the hawk. Still, it didn't seem to mind. The hawk dove lower for a closer look, so Rosco jumped as high as he could to scare it away. Finally, the hawk flew higher into the sky, but Rosco didn't stop barking. *Don't come back!* He warned with a nasty growl.

Just then, Mandy rounded the side of the house. "Rosco, what are you barking at?" she asked, concerned. Her eyes went to the baby chicks in the grass, chirping with fear, and she gasped. They were crowding together, trying to stay safe. She set the mash and water down quickly. "What are the chicks doing out here? Where's James? And what were you doing? Were you barking at them?"

I was chasing away a big, bad hawk before it stole one of them! Rosco thought, hoping Mandy would see the hawk. *Just look up at the sky, Mandy. You'll see.*

But she didn't look up. She only looked upset. She hurried over to them and put her arms protectively around them. "Rosco, you scared them! Thank goodness you didn't eat them!"

Uh-oh.

Rosco raced around the pen again and

barked, glancing up as he did, trying to make her understand. *I wouldn't eat them!*

"In the house—now!" She pointed to the door, just as James came back outside.

"What's going on?" James asked, concerned.

"You left the chicks out, James, and he tried to attack them!"

James' eyes shot wide when he saw the chicks outside of the pen.

Rosco's eyes shot wide, too. He hadn't tried to attack them!

"How could you do that, James? Where did you go?" asked Mandy.

"Mom needed help moving the table so she could mop the floor. I had to go and—"

"—He might've eaten them!"

James swallowed. "He was fine when I left, and I didn't leave them out! I put them back inside the coop." James ran to the gate to check and saw that indeed, it was open just enough for a chick to get out. "Oh, no."

Mandy hurried over for a look. "That was

very careless, James. We got lucky this time, but we'd better not trust him with the chickens from now on. Plus, who knows what he was doing the other night at the window? Maybe he was trying to scare them."

Rosco's heart sank.

"It was my fault. I'm so sorry." James frowned. "But you're right. We can't take any chances." He pointed to the doggie door, which was part of the kitchen door. "Inside, boy," he commanded.

Rosco gazed at James and then at Mandy with his most convincing, sad, puppy-eyed look. *Please try to understand. I was only trying to save them from the hawk.* How could he make them see? He glanced up at the sky again, but the hawk was gone.

"Go!" said James.

Rosco hung his head and trudged to his doggie door, then pushed it open and went inside.

He sat down on his bed. What was a dog to do? No one appreciated how he'd kept the baby chickens safe—twice! Worse, the kids thought he was trying to hurt them, and now, his little feathered friends were in more danger than the kids ever dreamed. He had to make James and Mandy understand, but that would be easier said than done.

CHAPTER 3
RULES, RULES RULES

A few days later, Rosco found himself sniffing at the sweet smell of flowers in the air and gazing up at the clear blue sky. Easter Sunday had finally arrived.

The kids had not made a big deal about the chicks again since the day the hawk had come, but they'd kept him inside the house whenever they'd gone out to play with the chicks.

It made him sad, but he brushed it off and focused on the beautiful morning. It wouldn't do any good to be upset today, after all. It would be much better just to enjoy the holiday.

He wagged his tail at the pleasant sound of the birds chirping in the trees. The Easter egg hunt would begin in just a few minutes. Rosco studied the rolling hillsides covered in grass and the lush green forest behind them.

Rosco followed as James and Mandy squeezed and elbowed their way through an enormous group of children at the park. They found a spot to wait, and he sat down on the grass. Dozens and dozens of kids—maybe even a hundred—dressed in their Sunday best, were chatting eagerly, waving baskets around, and exchanging tales of last year's incredible hunt.

Still, Rosco was anxious. James had filled him in about the rules for Easter all week. They'd said the Easter Bunny would bring him treats only if he were on his best behavior.

So he'd picked up his toys and dropped them in the bin so James didn't have to. He'd licked up the water and the crumbs that Mom had spilled on the kitchen floor, without being asked. He'd carried Mandy's backpack all the way home from the bus stop for her—in his teeth—twice this week.

Mandy had given him a lot of warnings about the holiday, too. "If you hear noises in the house on the night before Easter, it could be the Easter bunny, so don't bark!" At least that one had been easy. He'd fallen asleep early and hadn't heard a thing last night.

Fortunately, his hard work had paid off. He'd woken today to find that Mandy's basket contained a doggie treat with his name on it. It had been a fun Easter morning, watching the kids hunt for their baskets.

Unfortunately, it seemed there were more rules to be followed at the egg hunt today.

"Don't chase the rabbits," James had said. "They might be the Easter Bunny's helpers."

That might be very difficult, Rosco thought, because, after all, it was springtime, and rabbits were everywhere. Would it really hurt to chase them around now and then? It was one of his favorite things to do at the park. He wouldn't hurt them.

"If we find any candy, don't eat it," Mandy had warned. "It's bad for dogs."

Okay, so that would be easy. Candy wasn't his *thing.* On the other hand, if those plastic eggs were filled with hamburgers, things might be entirely different.

Rosco turned his attention to the field just in front of the crowd of children. Hundreds of plastic eggs had been scattered across the grass.

Rosco's mouth watered as he thought about how much he loved hard-boiled eggs. The kids had dyed loads of them yesterday with Mom and Dad.

"Look how easy it's going to be, Mandy," said James. "We're going to find so many eggs out there." He pointed toward the field full of color, and Rosco looked.

Mandy nodded with glee.

Rosco was startled as a boy nearby

turned to James and scowled. "Don't be so sure, kid." He was taller than James, but probably the same age, with brown hair.

James tightened his brow. "What do you mean? Why not?"

The boy laughed rudely. "You'll see."

Next to the unfriendly boy, a girl leaned forward. Rosco thought she might be the boy's twin. "Sometimes it's hard to hold onto all of your eggs out there. Better keep your wits about you." She stuck out her tongue and then slapped a high-five with her brother. They both snickered then slipped back into the crowd.

Rosco stopped panting. It didn't sound like *those* kids were on their best behavior today. Was anyone paying attention to the children that broke the rules?

Mandy turned to James, frowning. "What was that all about?"

James looked confused. "I don't know. They sure were rude, though."

Mandy nodded uncomfortably.

Rosco agreed. He shook it off and returned his attention to the glorious field of eggs.

The hunt was taking place in their Aunt Elizabeth's town, about an hour from their house, so they didn't know any of the other kids. Mom and Dad would be waiting with Aunt Elizabeth and the other parents near the entrance to the park when the hunt ended.

A few more minutes passed, and a man's voice came over the loudspeaker. "Attention, children! Grab your baskets—it's time for the Easter egg hunt to begin!"

"Here we go, Mandy. It's game time!" James grinned.

The announcer spoke again. "Happy Easter, everyone! Now, will all the children ages four and under please step forward?"

Little children in frilly springtime dresses or snappy slacks left the hands of their parents. They stepped onto the edges of the grassy field, Easter baskets in hand.

"They look so cute," Mandy said,

straightening her own Easter dress. "But what about us?"

"All right, youngsters," said the announcer, "when I say *go*, start gathering those eggs! Everyone else, please stay back."

Mandy looked at James, concerned. "The hunt is only for the little kids?"

James looked confused. "I guess so?"

"On your mark, get set, go!"

The toddlers and preschoolers rushed the field and set to work as Rosco looked on with dismay. "There won't be any eggs left for us," said Mandy quietly. She sounded worried.

"Maybe we're next?" James whispered.

Mandy shrugged. "I hope so."

Rosco hoped so, too.

The hunt lasted about fifteen minutes as the younger children filled their baskets with colored eggs, and parents snapped photos. When they'd cleared the field, the announcer's voice sounded over the speaker once more. "Thank you, everyone! I hope you enjoyed the mini hunt! And now, for our

main event! If I may have the attention of the older kids?"

The crowd of big kids went quiet. James and Mandy stood at attention, finally ready for their big moment.

"This egg hunt is for children ages five to ten."

James and Mandy looked at each other with relief.

"Hundreds of eggs have been hidden all over the park. Most of them contain jellybeans, but some are empty, and the empty ones will have the picture of a chocolate Easter bunny on the bottom. If you find one of these special eggs, you can turn them in at the end of the hunt to receive your very own chocolate Easter bunny!"

James glanced at Mandy, wide-eyed. "Wow!"

Mandy nodded back.

That's nice, thought Rosco. She and James both seemed to be big fans of chocolate bunnies, judging from their excitement at this morning's loot.

The announcer went on. "You'll have one hour to search for the eggs, and when the horn blows, that means it's time to come back."

CHAPTER 4
HUNTING DOG

A few minutes later, James and Mandy darted from rock to bush to tree checking for colored eggs. Rosco followed along until he noticed a flock of crows pecking at the grass in search of worms.

Without a second thought, he dashed after the birds. James and Mandy turned to look as the birds flapped their wings and took to the sky in what seemed like one great motion, leaving the dog racing in circles and barking from the field below. Rosco trotted back with his tongue hanging out.

"Rosco, you're not supposed to chase the birds!" Mandy called, ducking down to look under a bush. She grabbed a pink egg out from under it. "Don't you remember?"

Rosco panted. Mandy hadn't mentioned a thing about birds. He wouldn't have hurt them, though. He just liked to see them flap their wings, but she was right. He'd promised to be on his best behavior, and that apparently included not chasing crows. He would try harder.

"I think we need to keep him busy. Why don't we see if he can help us hunt for eggs?" Mandy said, kneeling down to check between some rocks. She held up a purple egg. "I found another one!" She turned the egg over, but there was no chocolate bunny pictured underneath. "Bummer." She shook it. "But it has jellybeans!" She dropped it inside her basket.

Hmm. Rosco thought. He could try to help.

"Cool!" James reached inside a flowerbed and pulled out a yellow egg. "I found one, too!" It didn't have a chocolate bunny on the bottom, either. He held it up. "Here, Rosco.

Come see this."

Rosco padded over to James. "Give it a sniff." He held the egg to Rosco's nose, and Rosco sniffed. "Now, go and hunt for these."

I can do that! Rosco panted. He would remember not to eat the candy, too.

Rosco continued on beside the kids as they made their way through the park, stopping to sniff through the beds of daffodils and rocks.

Every few seconds, one of the kids peeked beneath something, and every so often, one of them found an egg.

Next, they passed a hillside and a pond. Each of the kids found a few more eggs as they went.

Rosco stopped to stare at the ducks swimming in the pond. One waddled onto shore, and Rosco grinned. It looked so funny when it walked, but he remembered Mandy's warning: no birds. He watched for a few more seconds then turned away from the pond and raced to catch up to the kids.

Soon, the three of them passed some other kids, but it seemed the park was large enough that once the crowd split up, there was plenty of space to spread out.

A few minutes later, they approached the tall forest, and Rosco was surprised to see two little girls coming out of the woods looking upset. Had they been crying? Rosco noticed their baskets were empty. He panted and smiled at them, trying to make them smile back, but they sighed and looked away. Why did they look so sad?

Mandy glanced back at the girls and then to James. "I wonder what was wrong? Maybe there aren't any eggs left in there?" She pointed to the forest. "Maybe we shouldn't waste our time going in?"

James considered it. "The announcer said that the eggs were hidden in the whole park, though. There must be some left. Maybe they just didn't find any."

"Okay, maybe you're right." Mandy nodded. "I guess we ought to try."

CHAPTER 5
TROUBLE IN
THE WOODS

James peered up the trunk of a tall, leafy tree inside the forest, then glanced down at the base of it. Sure enough, a green egg sat there on the ground, well hidden beneath some ferns. He grabbed it and tossed it inside his basket then headed for a large boulder and looked underneath it—another egg! The forest seemed to be full of them. Why had the girls been crying? There was more than enough to go around.

"I found one!" Mandy called from the other side of the trail.

James looked around and saw Rosco sniffing at some rocks. He hadn't found any yet, but at least hunting this way might keep the dog out of trouble.

A few minutes passed, and James heard some twigs cracking on the ground. He looked up to see the twin brother and sister they'd spoken to before the hunt began. The twins stopped in the middle of the trail.

The boy glanced at Mandy standing among some bushes, then at James. "Well, if it isn't you two, again—redhead and his itty bitty baby sister."

James frowned. Why was this kid so unfriendly?

"Guess what?" the boy asked devilishly.

"What?" James narrowed his eyes. He didn't like his tone.

"It must be my lucky day because I just found a lot of eggs, all at once," said the boy, sounding a little too proud of himself.

James frowned. "What are you talking about?"

"Hand over your eggs," the boy demanded, holding out his hand.

"What?" James tightened his grip on his Easter basket and pulled it out of the boy's reach. "No way!" He noticed the boy's basket held more than twice as many colored eggs as James' basket did. Had he found that many already, or had he robbed *other* kids of their eggs?

"Do as he says," the twin sister said roughly.

Mandy shuffled over. "What's going on here?"

The boy spoke first. "It looks like your brother wants a piece of my fist." He set down the basket and pounded his fist against his other hand.

"He's trying to steal my eggs." James straightened his shoulders and tried to look tough.

The tall girl shook back her ponytails and stepped forward, straightening a large backpack that she wore over her shoulders. "He's not trying. He's succeeding. Now, hand them over, chump." She held out her hand.

"No way," said James. "Come on, Mandy. We're leaving." He glanced around for Rosco, but the dog was nowhere in sight. Too bad, because with one growl, Rosco could've sent the thieves packing.

Where was Rosco, anyway? All day, he'd been distracted with rabbits and birds. He'd really let them down this week. First the baby chicks, and now this. He'd better catch up soon.

Mandy huffed and stepped beside her brother, one hand planted firmly against her waist, the other gripping the handle of her basket.

The twin boy laughed at her. "You're a spunky one, aren't you?"

"Leave her alone," James said, his voice steady. "Come on, Mandy." He took a step forward to leave.

Without warning, the twin girl stuck her foot in front of James, but James didn't see it in time. He tripped, sailing forward. He threw his arms out in front of him and landed on his stomach with a thump.

The plastic eggs flew out of his basket in one unstoppable motion, and the basket rolled out of his reach. The twin sister rushed to gather up his eggs, stuffing them inside her backpack before James or Mandy had a chance to claim them.

"Hey! Those are mine!" James pulled himself to his feet. "Give them back!"

Mandy dropped her basket to help James.

"Nope," the girl said, grinning wickedly. "They were on the ground. I found them." She turned and hurried down the trail.

Before James could stop him, the twin boy grabbed Mandy's basket from the ground and emptied it into his. He let out an evil laugh and ran to catch up with his sister.

The boy turned around and waved a fist. "You'd better not follow us!"

James almost felt sick to his stomach as they disappeared from view. "Can you believe that?"

Mandy shook her head. "No, I can't! Every last one of our eggs—gone!"

James shook his head in disbelief.

"Are you okay, James? That was a nasty fall."

He looked at his clothes then brushed the dirt off his shirt and pants. "Yeah, I'm fine, but how did we let them get away with this? We have to go after them."

"No way, James. We don't know what they might do next. That boy seemed dangerous. So did the girl."

James picked up his basket, trying to control his anger. "How did I fall for that trick?"

"Should we go back and tell on them?" Mandy suggested. "They shouldn't get to keep all that candy."

James checked his watch. "No, they shouldn't, but I don't want to waste time. We only have thirty minutes left to find more eggs."

Mandy nodded and glanced at their

empty baskets. "And we have to start all over again," she said, her shoulders slumping.

"I know." James frowned. "I hope we can still find a few."

"I'll bet they stole the eggs from those girls we saw," said Mandy. "No wonder they were crying."

Just then, Rosco skipped out of the woods from the other direction.

"Rosco!" Mandy called. "Where have you been? We really needed you a few minutes ago. Plus, we told you not to run off without us!"

Rosco drew his eyebrows in sadly and drooled. He opened his mouth. Out plopped a blue egg.

"He found an egg!" Mandy picked it up and turned it over. "And look—there's a chocolate bunny on the bottom!"

"Really?" James took the egg from Mandy to look. "Wow. Good boy, Rosco!"

At least something was going right. Rosco panted and sat down.

"Here, you can have it, Mandy."

Mandy waved it away. "No way, James. You keep it. At least they didn't trip me." She glanced at the dirty knees of his slacks.

"Okay, thanks, Mandy." James said. "But if we find another chocolate bunny egg, it's yours."

"Okay. Deal." Mandy nodded. "Let's tell Mom and Dad and Aunt Elizabeth about those kids when we get back, but for now, let's get back to hunting for eggs."

"That sounds like a good plan." James nodded, and Mandy followed him further into the forest.

"Come on, Rosco," she called.

CHAPTER 6
MUDDY WATERS

Soon, Rosco was leading the hunt. He sniffed at the mossy forest floor and sniffed at the wild flowers in bloom, and soon, he'd found two eggs for the kids.

"Good job!" said Mandy. She put one in her basket, and James took the other.

Rosco wagged his tail and left James and Mandy to search another section of the woods, close by. After all, there were more colorful eggs to be found, and they'd be smart to spread out.

But Mandy's words were troubling him. What had he missed earlier? Why had Mandy said they'd needed him?

Rosco slowed down when he smelled

more jellybeans because that meant an Easter egg was nearby. He stopped to sniff, when out of nowhere a huge butterfly flew up and landed on his nose. *Cheeky fellow!* He shook his head until the butterfly flew off.

He watched as the butterfly landed on a nearby flower. He glanced around, and soon, his eyes rested upon a squirrel. The little brown critter stood tall on a rock and stayed completely still.

Chasing squirrels was Rosco's *other* favorite thing to do at a park. He glanced in the direction of Mandy and James. They wouldn't notice, would they? Besides, they'd said nothing about chasing squirrels today. It wasn't a rabbit *or* a bird, after all. They probably wouldn't mind.

He took off at a sprint, focusing on the creature's fluffy little tail. The squirrel dashed away. He chased it high and low, around trees, over rocks, and past wildflowers, until he heard Mandy's voice.

"Rosco! Where are you?" she called from

a distance.

Rosco stopped, and the squirrel darted up a tree. Rosco turned and ran in the direction of Mandy's voice, but he didn't see the puddle in front of him until it was too late.

He splashed across the puddle, sending cold, muddy water high into the air. On the other side, he stopped to shake himself off and noticed the dirt speckling his legs. He licked his chops and tasted mud. It was on his face, too. *Uh-oh. They're not going to like this.* He picked up his pace and hurried back to the kids.

"Where did you run off to, this time, Rosco?" Mandy scolded him as he approached.

Rosco hung his head as he reached her.

"Oh, my goodness!" Mandy cried as he came closer. "What happened, Rosco? Your fur is filthy. Mom's not going to like that!"

Rosco made a sad face. *I didn't see the puddle in time.* He was very sorry.

"Why aren't you following the rules today, Rosco?" she asked. "What's gotten into you lately?"

James sighed. "Can't you stay out of trouble, boy, just this once? I mean—it's Easter Sunday."

Mandy shook her head with disappointment. James did the same.

Rosco sighed heavily and trudged behind them. How had he managed to cause more trouble? He'd only wanted to have a little fun. How were they ever going to trust him again? First, the baby chicks, and now, this.

Just then, Rosco looked up to see two boys who looked to be about Mandy's age running toward them, huffing and puffing. The boys stopped when they reached James and Mandy.

The first one caught his breath. "Look out if you're going that way, because there's a pair of kids stealing eggs from people." He pointed in the direction that James and Mandy were headed. He held up an empty basket. "They stole ours and a bunch of other kids' eggs!"

The second boy caught his breath, nodding to agree with him. "They were really mean!"

"That happened to us, too!" said James. "What did the kids look like?"

"A boy and a girl, really tall," said the first boy. "Brown hair. They looked like they're probably brother and sister."

"Yep, it's the same kids," said James, frowning.

Uh-oh, thought Rosco. What was this about? And what did James mean, *it happened to us?* Was that what Rosco had missed? How had he missed something so important?

Mandy pushed some of her long, brown hair behind her ear. "We've got enough eggs now—maybe we should go report them before this gets any worse?"

James sighed heavily. "But we still have a little time before the horn blows. I think we should stop them, ourselves, before they steal any more eggs. Besides, we all deserve to leave with the eggs we found. If we don't do anything, they might get away before the grownups can stop them." James looked at the boys, who seemed to agree.

Rosco straightened his shoulders and waited for instructions. *Whatever it takes, James! I'm here for you.*

But James didn't ask for Rosco's help. Neither did Mandy. Maybe Rosco needed to get their attention. He sat down at James' feet and made a serious face. *At your service, James.* But James only looked at the other kids. Was he just distracted or was he ignoring Rosco on purpose?

"We'll help you," said the first boy. "My name's Joshua, and this is Jake, by the way."

Mandy and James introduced themselves.

"How are we going to stop them? They scared me." Mandy hesitated. "That boy made it clear that he'd punch you, James."

Punch him? thought Rosco, shocked. *I won't let anyone punch James, or anyone else!*

James shook his head. "I'm going to reason with him. Besides, if they try anything, we outnumber them."

"Are you sure?" asked Mandy.

"I'm sure," said James.

Rosco would add even more strength and power to the mix. Still, James and Mandy hadn't yet asked for his help.

James turned his attention to Joshua and Jake again. "Can you show us where they are?"

Both boys nodded with enthusiasm.

"Follow me," said Jake. I'll take you to them."

Rosco followed quietly as the group crept further through the forest. Finally, they came to a cluster of bushes and hunched down behind so they wouldn't be noticed.

"Look—over there," whispered Joshua. He pointed to a stone bridge that crossed a small stream. James and the others looked.

On the other side of the bridge, Rosco recognized the rude boy and girl who'd been in the crowd of children before the hunt started. They were stuffing their faces with jellybeans. So those were the troublemakers?

"Okay, I see them," James whispered.

"Look how full of eggs that backpack is!" said Mandy. "I wonder how many kids they've stolen eggs from by now?"

Rosco nudged James with his nose. The eggs were in the backpack?

"Hey Rosco, I'm sorry, but I can't be sure you'll listen," said James. "So you stay back, boy. And don't run away this time, please."

"For once..." Mandy whispered.

Rosco stared at James and then Mandy, shocked. *You really don't want my help?* he thought. He looked at Mandy. *Have I been that bad?*

"Now, here's what we're going to do," James said. The kids huddled together as he explained the plan.

Rosco sat outside the group, with a sinking feeling in his stomach. *But James, I can help...*

CHAPTER 7
JUSTICE IS SERVED

James took a deep breath and marched across the bridge, one hand firmly gripping his basket, the other clenched tightly. He wasn't going to start a fight, but he would make sure that justice was served.

Mandy, Jake, and Joshua followed him bravely. James glanced back and saw that Rosco sat alone, watching and waiting at the far end of the bridge. The dog had listened, for once. Thank goodness. They certainly didn't need any more mischief from him today.

James set his eyes upon the twins at the other side of the bridge and wiped the sweat from his brow. If the plan didn't work, he wasn't sure what they'd do.

"What's this?" the twin brother said with a sneer as James and the others approached. "You're back? Don't you understand how this works? We take your eggs, and you run off and cry."

The boy set his basket full of eggs on the ground and smacked a fist against his hand, just like he'd done earlier. The twin sister crossed her arms and planted her feet wide.

James straightened his shoulders. "Look, we don't want any trouble. We just want our eggs back. Give us back the eggs, and we'll leave you alone."

"And if we don't?" The twin sister snapped her gum. "Then what? Are you threatening us?"

James stared at them hard. "I'm not threatening anyone. I just want to give you a chance to do the right thing."

The twin brother laughed. "We're gonna do whatever we want, and what we *want* is to keep the eggs." He glanced around James' shoulder at Jake, Joshua, and Mandy. "They're just a bunch of little kids you've got there, anyway. You think we're scared?"

His twin sister chuckled. "Guess what? We're not."

James took a step forward. "Give us back our eggs," he demanded. They weren't being reasonable—at all. He'd have to think fast.

Just then, the sound of a horn blared from a distance. The kids looked around, unsure what to do.

Jake hollered from behind James. "Those are our eggs! We found them. You stole them!"

"And we're not *little*!" shouted Joshua.

Mandy called boldly. "It's over! This is your last chance before we tell the announcer what you did!"

The twin brother punched his fist again. "I warned you not to threaten me. Who's first?" He snarled. "Come and get it." He put up his fists, ready for a fight.

His sister looked worried. "The hunt's

over. Let's get out of here. These losers aren't worth it." She scanned the area, probably looking for the easiest escape route. Her brother glanced at her for a moment. "I'm not going to stand here and take this from these little punks."

James furrowed his brow and set his basket down. This was going to be more difficult than he'd thought.

***

Rosco had watched from afar. Maybe the twins hadn't noticed him.

James had told Rosco not to get involved, and he'd listened, but this was getting out of control. He couldn't just stand by and watch things get worse. The bad kids might escape with all those eggs, or worse, someone might get hurt.

No, Rosco couldn't stay out of it any longer. *Sorry, James, but I have to help.* Without warning, he raced toward the group,

dashing around James. Both twins froze.
With a growl, Rosco soared at the twin girl's
shoulder and grabbed the strap of her
backpack in his teeth. He'd carried Mandy's
schoolbooks home all week—this was easy.

Rosco turned and ran toward James,
dropping the backpack triumphantly at
James' feet. Still, it wasn't over. He headed
back toward the twin boy and growled, then
let out an angry bark.

The boy looked nervous and took a step

back. "Nice doggie?" he said cautiously.

Too late for that, thought Rosco, grasping the handle of the Easter basket with his teeth until it tipped over. He watched as the stolen eggs poured out in every direction like a sea of color, and the kids rushed forward to collect them.

He heard the kids cheer as James poured the eggs out of the backpack and tossed the backpack aside.

"Good boy, Rosco!" cried Mandy. "What a good boy you are! Thanks!"

"What a dog!" said Jake. Joshua patted Rosco on the back before he stooped down to collect some eggs from the ground.

Rosco looked up to see the twins dash down the trail, out of sight. *Good riddance.*

Another small crowd of children, who'd been heading back at the sound of the horn, stopped to find out what had happened.

"They stole from us, too!" a little girl cried.

"Come and take back your eggs, then!"

Mandy replied.

Rosco watched the crowd of children collecting their eggs, and noticed that they were all sharing. Peace had been restored. *Whew.*

James came over and reached out to pet Rosco. "Wow, Rosco, I'm glad you decided to help. You really saved the day! I'm sorry I ever doubted you. Thanks, boy!"

Rosco licked his hand. *You're welcome, James! No problem!*

A few minutes later, back at the entrance, the kids lined up with excitement to turn in the special eggs they'd found containing marks on the bottom.

Mandy reached out and accepted her prize. "A chocolate bunny! Thank you!" She held it up. "Look, Aunt Elizabeth!"

James and Mandy had told their aunt and their parents everything that had happened, and they, in turn, had informed the hunt's organizers about the troublemaking twins. Rosco watched from a distance as the twins were scolded by a man who appeared to be the twins' father. *Let's hope they've learned their lesson,* he thought.

James unwrapped his bunny and took a bite of the chocolate ears. "Tastes even better than it looks."

"I'll bet it does," said Aunt Elizabeth. "Well, you certainly earned it!"

"Someone else earned a treat, too." Mom pulled a dog biscuit from her purse. "Here you go, Rosco!" She threw it, and Rosco jumped up into the air and caught it. "Good boy!"

"Happy Easter, Rosco!" Mandy called.

Rosco smiled and panted.

CHAPTER 8

CREATURES OF THE NIGHT

Later that evening, after a delicious Easter dinner at Aunt Elizabeth's house and a long drive home, Rosco and the kids were tired. Mom called from the hallway. "Time for bed, kids! It's getting late!"

James and Mandy changed into their pajamas and brushed their teeth. Easter day had been so much fun. Rosco let out a big yawn.

Oh, what a week it had been! Rosco waited until the kids shut their doors, then headed downstairs and settled in on his doggie bed.

Rosco had been minding his manners,

following rules, and trying his best to help the kids as much as possible this week. He'd helped them stop the bullies in the forest, and James and Mandy seemed to trust him again—thank goodness—but they still thought he was a danger to the new baby chicks.

How was he ever going to convince the kids that he was only interested in protecting the chicks?

Rosco got up from his bed and checked outside, peering into the darkness. A pale moon lit the yard, and a soft wind blew, but all was quiet. The chicks must be sleeping. Would they be safe from the creatures of the night?

He yawned again and settled back down on his bed. He was fast asleep in minutes.

Hours later, he woke to the distant howling of coyotes. It wasn't unusual to hear the coyotes in the middle of the night because they were most active after dark, hunting for their meals. Still, he'd better be sure there weren't any coyotes in the yard.

He padded over to a window and stared out into the darkness. Shadows from the trees and bushes seemed to dance in the soft wind.

The howling finally stopped, but what was that? Rosco strained his ears and heard a scratching sound. It seemed to be coming from the far end of the yard, where the coop was. *Something's out there!* He peered through the glass and saw a large, four-legged creature moving around in the dark. *Ah ha!* The coyote was back, and it was scratching at the chicken coop!

Rosco choked back a bark. Mom, Dad, James, and Mandy would not be happy if he woke them in the middle of the night, especially after such a busy holiday.

They would also not be happy if the coyote broke into the chicken coop and gobbled up their little yellow friends, however. He had to alert the family. He had no choice. He let out a booming yelp to wake them. "Woof, woof, woof!"

Still, he had to stop the coyote! Was he too late already? He dashed through his doggie door and raced across the backyard, hoping with all his might that he could reach the chicks in time.

And there it was—the coyote! It sniffed and scratched at the coop. The poor chicks must be terrified! Rosco barked fiercely, and the beastly figure dashed off into the darkness without so much as a glance. Rosco sighed with relief, panting.

A few moments later, Mom and Dad rushed outside in their pajamas, with James and Mandy close on their heels.

"What is it, Rosco?" Dad called, hurrying across the grass. "What happened?"

James ran ahead of him and reached Rosco first. "Look, Dad! Claw marks!" He pointed at the side of the little red hen house. "Something was here! What do you think it was?"

It was a coyote! Rosco thought, wishing he could tell them. A big one, with sharp teeth and long legs, scratching its claws against the wooden planks of the coop.

He paced alongside the pen, sniffing for traces of the animal.

Mandy stepped inside the pen, unlocked the gate to the coop, and peeked inside. She counted the chicks. "They're safe. Thank goodness!" she said, shutting the gate and locking it tightly.

Dad examined the scratch marks. "Wow, it must've been a coyote. This coop is very strong, so I don't think it could've gotten in, but Rosco must've stopped it before it had the chance to try."

"Really?" Mandy's eyes were wide. "So Rosco was trying to protect the chicks?"

"Yes, it looks that way," said Mom.

Dad squatted down, searching for footprints.

Mandy studied Rosco's face. "So maybe we *should* listen to him when he barks? We were wrong not to want Rosco's help with the twins at the egg hunt. Maybe we've been wrong about Rosco when it comes to the chickens, too?"

Rosco grinned at her. *You have been wrong! I only want them to be safe.*

"I wonder if that's what he heard the other night when we thought he was barking for no reason?" James glanced around. "A coyote?"

"I'll bet it was," said Dad. "Coyotes can be very quiet, but Rosco probably would've heard if one came into our yard. Dogs can hear a lot better than we can, after all."

Rosco couldn't stop grinning. He sat down and panted. They finally understood!

"Wow, then that means Rosco saved the chickens—more than once!" said Mandy, reaching out to pet his soft ears. "Good boy, Rosco. I'm sorry I ever doubted you."

"Me, too," said James.

No problem, kids. Rosco panted and smiled, so happy to be understood.

Rosco would keep watch, and the chicks would be safe. The kids had nothing to worry about, as long as they let him do his job. He'd never let them down.

Mandy reached out and hugged him. "Thanks, Rosco! You're the best dog ever!"

"Ruff, ruff!" said Rosco.

Happy Easter from Rosco the Rascal!

THE END

The Author

Shana Gorian, originally from western Pennsylvania, lives in Southern California with her husband and two children, and the real *Rosco*, their German shepherd.

The Illustrators

Deidre Gorian is the talented daughter of the author. She has been drawing since she was a young child and especially enjoys drawing her dog. She completed all of the interior black-and-white chapter illustrations for this book.

Josh Addessi is a quirky illustrator and animation professor based in Northwest Indiana who illustrates the covers for the Rosco the Rascal series. He has digitally painted all manner of book covers, stage backdrops, and trading cards.

Rosco the Rascal

The *real* Rosco is every bit as loveable and rascally as the fictional Rosco. He loves hunting for Easter eggs and running laps around chicken coops, and he definitely likes hamburgers more than jellybeans.

Visit **shanagorian.com** and sign up for her email list to be notified of new releases, and join Rosco the Rascal for more adventures in these full-length books:

Rosco the Rascal Visits the Pumpkin Patch
Rosco the Rascal In the Land of Snow
Rosco the Rascal Goes to Camp
Rosco the Rascal at the St. Patrick's Day Parade
Rosco the Rascal and the Holiday Lights
Rosco the Rascal's Ghost Town Adventure
Calendar Dog, Spring & Summer
Calendar Dog, Fall & Winter
Audiobook: Series Collection, Books 1-5
Audiobook: Series Collection, Books 6-10

17862615R00043